THE PIRATE KING

BLOODBOAR
THE
BURIED DOOM

With special thanks to J N Richards

To Toby Saunders

www.beastquest.co.uk

ORCHARD BOOKS
338 Euston Road, London NW1 3BH
Orchard Books Australia
Level 17/207 Kent St, Sydney, NSW 2000

A Paperback Original
First published in Great Britain in 2011

Beast Quest is a registered trademark of Beast Quest Limited
Series created by Working Partners Limited, London

Text © Beast Quest Limited 2011
Inside illustrations by Pulsar Estudio (Beehive Illustration)
Cover illustrations by Steve Sims © Orchard Books 2011

A CIP catalogue record for this book is available from
the British Library.

ISBN 978 1 40831 315 2

5 7 9 10 8 6 4

Printed in Great Britain by CPI Bookmarque

Orchard Books is a division of Hachette Children's Books,
an Hachette UK company

www.hachette.co.uk

BLOODBOAR
THE
BURIED DOOM

BY ADAM BLADE

TH

WESTERN OCEAN

THE FOREST
OF FEAR

THE

THE RUBY DESERT

SPI

Tremble, warriors of Avantia, for a new enemy stalks your land!

I am Sanpao, the Pirate King of Makai! My ship brings me to your shores to claim an ancient magic more powerful than any you've encountered. Nothing will stand in my way, especially not that pathetic boy Tom, or his friends. Even Aduro cannot help you this time. My pirate band will pillage and burn without mercy, and my Beasts will be more than a match for any hero in Avantia.

Pirates! Batten down the hatches and raise the sails. We come to conquer and destroy!

Sanpao the Pirate King

PROLOGUE

"Do you think he will he ever wake up?"

King Hugo looked down at Aduro who lay as still as a corpse in one of the infirmary's sick beds. His skin was yellow and creased like parchment.

"I hope so, sire," Taladon replied. "But he's been in this deep slumber for many days now – it took all his magic to throw off Sanpao's spell." Taladon's face was shaded with a mixture of pride and sorrow.

"Any other wizard would have died."

King Hugo sighed. "Without Aduro's magic, we must gather men to protect our kingdom. Tom has sent a messenger from the Icy Plains with Storm and Blizzard. Sanpao and his pirates will be on their way. We must get ready for battle—"

The long, low wail of a war-horn interrupted the king.

"We're under attack!" Taladon cried.

King Hugo swept out of the palace infirmary, with Taladon following close behind. They hurried to the top of the city walls where several archers stood on the ramparts, staring at the southern horizon.

In the distance, King Hugo could see a Beast with a huge body charging towards Avantia's city walls. The Beast's legs were thick with muscle and they kicked up dust clouds, his massive hooves leaving deep grooves in the land. "Sanpao has sent a Beast to test us," King Hugo growled.

The Beast came to a thundering stop as he reached a small settlement of huts just outside the gates of the city. Sunlight glinted from two wickedly sharp tusks that curved out from the Beast's warty face. Froth poured from his massive jaws. Rows of spikes jutted out of his body. He tossed his head from side to side, and small, mean eyes raked his surroundings.

King Hugo felt a stab of fear. "He's going to attack the village. We have to stop this!" He turned to his archers. "Release your arrows."

"Wait, sire. It won't work," Taladon

said. "I know this Beast: it's
Bloodboar, the Buried Doom." He
pointed. "Look at his back and head,
there's no way an arrow will be able
to pierce that armour."

A bone casing covered the Beast's
thick bristly body, almost as if the
creature's skeleton had grown on
the outside.

The Beast gave a roar, dipped his
head and charged one of the wooden

huts in the village, ripping it up with his tusks. Men, women and children ran screaming from the Beast as it crashed into another wooden house, skewering the door on his tusks, before throwing the shack over his head.

The villagers ran towards Avantia's city walls.

The king turned to his men. "Those villagers need refuge. Get them within the city walls and raise the

drawbridge." Some archers sped off.

King Hugo could hear the Beast grunting with joy each time he destroyed a hut, his tusks ripping at wood. He hoped Bloodboar would be distracted long enough for the villagers to get to safety.

In minutes, the village was a pile of rubble. Bloodboar turned to face the towering walls of Avantia and gave a bellow of rage as the last of the villagers ran inside the city. The drawbridge slammed shut.

Taladon called to the Avantian soldiers. "Grab your weapons!"

King Hugo looked back at the Beast. Bloodboar was pawing at the ground and surveying the walls, as if he was trying to work out if he could force his way inside.

"He's going to try and ram his way

in," said an archer, fearfully.

King Hugo smiled as he felt
confidence surge through him.
"Let him try. The walls are solid."

"Sire," Taladon said, with a frown.
"Bloodboar is one of the cleverest
Beasts to have lived. Who knows
what his next move will be?"

Bloodboar gave a deep, throaty
roar and then stabbed his huge tusks
into the ground just in front of the
city walls. He began to burrow,
shovelling dirt away from the base.

"He's going to dig his way in!"
Taladon cried.

From behind them, came an
ear-splitting *crack*. Taladon and King
Hugo whipped round. At the centre
of the city's courtyard, stone pavings
were falling away into a chasm that
had appeared in the ground. Out of

the hole burst forth an enormous tree. Its golden branches reached up eagerly to the sky, and emerald green leaves unfurled swiftly.

The Tree of Being.

"At our hour of deepest peril, the Tree has chosen to come to the heart of Avantia," King Hugo murmured. "It must be protected, for the sake of everyone in the kingdom."

The scrape and crash of Bloodboar's ferocious digging echoed around them.

King Hugo and Taladon stared into each other's faces.

"Sanpao and his pirates will be here soon," King Hugo said. "And Bloodboar needs to be stopped. How will we do both?"

"Tom and Elenna must get back to the city, or all hope will be lost." Taladon said. Tom had already sent

a message ahead with a blind boy
called Abel, telling the king and his
father to get ready.

King Hugo stared round at his
kingdom. "Avantia is in grave danger."
A lump formed in his throat. By day's
end, the fate of everyone in the city
would be decided. *We need you, Tom*,
he thought. *Like never before.*

CHAPTER ONE

WARRIORS IN DISGUISE

Tom risked a glance over the side of the flying pirate ship, a *whoosh* of cold air stinging his cheeks. Below, he could see the Avantian landscape sliding by – mountains, valleys, lakes and forests all blurring into each other. Tom had seen so many different lands on his Quests. The beautiful landscapes of Gwildor and

Tavania, and the strange, dark world of Gorgonia. But Avantia was the only place he'd ever call home, and he'd risk anything to save it.

I'm disguised as a pirate and stowed away on a boat filled with my enemies, he thought. *This is about as dangerous as it gets.*

The mountains where Tom had fought his previous Quest were a long way from King Hugo's palace. Sneaking aboard was the only way to reach the city at the same time as Sanpao.

Tom looked over at Elenna, who was sitting behind the ship's storehouse. She met his glance and nodded over to a group of pirates who were a few sword lengths away from them. They were busy sharpening their weapons and practising their sword strokes. They thrust their blades into straw bales, in time to a pirate song:

"*Parry, duck, thrust and slice,*

Hack them down, don't think twice."

"They fight well," Elenna mouthed.

"So do we," Tom replied, crouching low as he came to sit beside her.

Elenna gave a tense smile. "That's true, but they outnumber us twenty to one. There's no way we could win a fight against them."

Tom shuddered, suddenly cold in his stolen pirate clothes. He watched Sanpao join the pirates' training and show them a vicious move with his battleaxe. The pirate king's tattooed body was roped with muscle, and a glistening, oiled plait hung down his back, with barbs of iron jutting out from it. If Sanpao discovered them on board...

"Don't worry," he said, as confidently as he could. "No one will see through our disguise, we're—"

"Oi, you!" a pirate with a matted beard snarled, looming over them. "What do you think you're doing here?"

Tom stiffened, his hand immediately dropping to the sword at his waist.

The pirate pointed at them with a meaty finger. "Get off your backsides and help fix the rigging on the mainsail."

They jumped to their feet, Tom being careful to keep his face lowered. He couldn't risk the pirate recognising him.

"We'll get right to it," Elenna barked in her best pirate voice.

The bandit nodded. "That's the spirit, laddie."

Tom had to swallow down a laugh.

They strode towards the mainsail, but Tom felt an odd vibration at his hip. He dug into his pocket and his fingers crept over the Eye of Kronus – the token that he'd won from the last Beast. Normally, he would have kept the eye on the fur sash that magically appeared when his jewelled belt was stolen by Aduro. But Tom knew he couldn't risk wearing this latest token in full view of the pirates in case they recognised it. The eye felt cold and slimy and danced in his palm as it vibrated once again. Tom quickly scanned the area to make sure no one was watching before taking the token out. The eye was cloudy as he peered down at it.

A dull red light flooded over its surface and then faded to reveal a vision of a familiar figure. Taladon!

Tom frowned. He could see his father shaking hands with Sanpao. *But my father would never shake Sanpao's hand! The Pirate King is our enemy.* He peered even more closely – only to see Sanpao plunge a knife into Taladon's chest. Tom bit down on his lip to stop himself from crying out.

Elenna touched his arm. "What's wrong," she asked.

Tom was shaking but forced himself to tell her what he'd seen. "It can't be true," Tom finished. "My father can't die." He felt the eye vibrate in his

palm again and then it burst into a shower of transparent gel. Tom wiped his hand on his rough pirate clothes and took a deep, steadying breath. In the past, the tokens he had won from the defeated Beasts had always helped him. The Eye of Kronus had to be doing the same. "This must be a warning – a warning about something that might happen," Tom said. "Well, I won't let it!"

"Quit all that yammering, and get that knot out of the rigging," the pirate with the beard yelled at them from the other side of the deck.

Tom and Elenna hastily moved to work at the knot.

"I don't want to worry you," Elenna whispered. "But what if you can't stop that future from happening? Or what if it has happened already?"

Tom shook his head. "My father won't die." He thumped his chest with a fist. "Whilst there's blood in my veins, I will not allow Sanpao to kill him."

Elenna nodded. "Then we need to be ready. If Sanpao wants to kill Taladon, it's down to us to stop him."

Tom's friend was right. He opened his mouth to respond but stopped as he saw something fast and sharp whizzing through the air towards them. An arrow!

CHAPTER TWO

RAINING ARROWS

"WATCH OUT!" Tom yelled, leaping in front of his friend and raising his shield. The arrow thunked into the wood, making Tom's arm shake.

Elenna had dropped to the deck and she got shakily to her feet. "Thanks, Tom," she managed to gasp.

Tom pulled the arrow from his shield. It was fluted with red and gold feathers. Avantain colours.

"Arm yourselves!" the pirate with the matted beard cried, running up to them, his cutlass drawn. "We're near Avantia's city walls. King Hugo's archers are trying to shoot us down! But we're going to crush them, you'll see."

Tom released his sword, even as he felt his chest tighten. He didn't like being on this side of the battle. It felt wrong.

"My weapon's in the storehouse," Elenna growled in her pirate voice. "I'll have to go and get it."

The pirate grinned and showed blackened teeth. "Quick sharp, laddie."

The two friends darted between Sanpao's men, who were all running to take up a position at the ship's rail. Elenna and Tom ducked behind the storehouse. "We need to get off this ship," Elenna panted.

"But how?" Tom asked "We're a long way from the ground."

"We'll do what Sanpao and his pirates did on the ice plains," Elenna said, her eyes lighting up. "Grab one of the lifeboats and lower it down."

Tom grinned. "Let's go!"

Keeping low, Tom and Elenna hurried across the deck to the lifeboats, which rested by the side of the ship. The boats were attached to thick ropes which ran through a crude pulley system. Tom and Elenna swiftly worked to lower a vessel overboard. Jumping into it, they loosened the ropes so that the boat began sinking down and down... As Tom eased open a knot in the rope, he heard a whistling sound.

Instinctively, he threw himself forward and an arrow flew right past where his head had been moments before.

"Tom!" Elenna cried. "Are you alright?"

"I'm fine," Tom insisted, looking around him at the rain of arrows that showered Sanpao's ship from the king's archers. He made a decision. "We're too far away to tell King Hugo's soldiers who we really are. Besides, Sanpao's men would hear us. You've got to finish lowering the boat. I'll cover us with my sheild."

Elenna quickly grabbed the trailing end of rope, unravelled the knot, and fed it through the pulley. As the boat dropped like a stone through the air, Tom stood in front of his friend using his sword to bat away the arrows that

whizzed towards them. The sound
of his blade connecting with the
arrowheads clanged all around them
and sparks flew up from his sword
until it shone red. In his other hand
he held up his shield, and his arm
hummed with tension as arrows
slammed into the wood.

The land was gradually rising up to meet them and the walls of Avantia were now in view. Tom crouched slightly to keep his balance in the swiftly lowering boat. They were going to land within running distance of the city. He just hoped he and Elenna could get inside the walls in time to help keep Sanpao out.

They were near the ground when their lifeboat came to a shuddering halt. Tom looked up at the pulley and saw Sanpao and two of his men holding the rope and pulling the boat back up to the deck. The Pirate King's scarred face was twisted with rage as he stared at Tom and spotted his shield.

Their game was up.

"Tom, they've found us," Elenna cried. "What are we going to do?"

"We take a chance," Tom replied. He sheathed his sword and looked down at his shield. There were several tokens set into the wood but it was the white feather that he was interested in. "Hold onto me. We're going to jump out of this boat and use Arcta's feather to fly into the city."

"Tom, the feather can't support both of us," Elenna protested. "We'll—"

Tom didn't let Elenna finish her sentence. Instead he pulled her in close, lifted his shield over their heads, and leapt over the side of the small boat. Elenna clung to him as they floated through the air.

"You'd better hide, Tom," Sanpao cried after them. "Because I'm going to find you and when I do you'll be sorry."

Tom floated through the air. He was close to the walls of the city now and could see the faces of the Avantian archers. Their expressions were grim as they pulled back their bowstrings and aimed towards him. Arrows whizzed past Tom and Elenna, some so close they sliced tears in their clothes.

Tom angled his body and weaved in and out of the arrows until they were within shouting distance of the archers on the city walls.

"It's Tom and Elenna," he cried as they floated towards the battlements that surrounded the king's palace. "Stop shooting!"

The archers lowered their bows, their faces lighting up with recognition.

Tom kicked out as they came to an

open window in the palace and
they dived through, rolling onto
a flagstone floor. Tom crashed into
something hard and solid, and gave
a pained gasp as the air was knocked
out of him.

Climbing to his feet, Tom realised that he had smashed into a golden chair. They were in King Hugo's throne room! As he helped Elenna up, the door was flung open and King Hugo and Taladon charged into the chamber.

"Thank goodness you're here!" King Hugo said. "Follow me. We can't hold off Sanpao and the Pirates of Makai for much longer."

Tom's eyes met his father's. He felt relief flood through him. The last time he had seen Taladon, he had been gravely ill. Now, he looked tired and his chest was bound with rough bandages, but he was alive.

"It's good to see you, son," Taladon said, his voice breaking.

"Come on. Let's go!" Tom said, after briefly hugging his father.

Tom and Elenna followed King Hugo and Taladon as they raced out to the battlements. Tom gasped as he saw that that the Tree of Being had appeared in the middle of the courtyard. It pulsed with energy and bathed everything in warm light.

But then the tree shuddered. Tom could hear a deep, rhythmic thumping sound coming from the south side of the city, making the whole courtyard shake. "What's that noise?" he asked.

"Sanpao has sent a Beast, Bloodboar, to breach the city walls by digging under them," Taladon explained.

Tom felt a thrill of fear that hardened into determination. Pirates on one side, a Beast on the other. This was a challenge like no other!

CHAPTER THREE

THE ARMOURED BEAST

Arriving on top of the city walls, Tom and Elenna could see that Sanpao's ship had retreated. It hovered in the air. The pirates were watching the palace.

Some of the archers pulled back their bowstring as far as they could go but released arrows didn't even get close to reaching the ship.

"Archers," King Hugo called "Save your arrows."

At the prow of the ship, Tom could see the muscular outline of Sanpao, his battleaxes strapped to his back. His oiled plait curled in the air like a snake as the wind snapped and roared all around him.

The Pirate King raised a war horn made of bone to his lips and his voice boomed out towards them.

"Give me the Tree of Being," Sanpao demanded, in a voice as sharp as a blade. "There is no need for any more bloodshed."

King Hugo shook his head. "Never!"

"Give it to me," Sanpao snarled "Or I will unleash the full power of Bloodboar."

Tom turned to his king. "Sire,

leave Bloodboar to Elenna and I."

King Hugo nodded. Taladon looked solemnly at Tom. "This Beast is clever and vicious," he warned. "You will need your wits and strength. Fight well."

"My mother's life depends on me winning," Tom replied. Freya was trapped in Gwildor until Tom could defeat Sanpao and use the Tree of Being to get back to her. "I won't let either of you down."

Tom and Elenna raced down the stairs from the battlements. As they reached the courtyard they could see a throng of soldiers, swords drawn, standing at the south wall. Cracks had appeared all across the surface and a massive tusk rammed through the wall, its razor-sharp tip piercing a soldier's side. The soldier screamed and fell to the floor. With panicked cries the soldier's friends dragged the injured man away.

"Stand back," Tom cried, pushing his way to the front. "Elenna and I will fight this Beast."

Two tusks slammed through the wall and then, in an explosion of rock, Bloodboar burst into the courtyard. Tiny stone fragments slashed at their skin and Tom could

hear the soldiers behind them scrambling backwards.

Sanpao's voice echoed into the courtyard. "Bloodboar – uproot the Tree of Being and bring it to me."

Tom lowered his hands and stared at the Beast. Bloodboar was huge, his torso thick with muscle. Two tusks jutted out of his face and his jaw was lined with teeth that looked jagged and lethal. A row of spikes sprouted from the Beast's body.

Tom felt a wave of fear crash over him but he tried to fight against it. He pointed his sword at Bloodboar. "If you want the Tree, you'll have to defeat me first!" he cried.

"Me too," Elenna added.

Bloodboar's nostrils flared with anger, his yellow eyes glowing fiercely from beneath the panels of armour that covered his head and body. The white protective casing glistened like bone in the sunlight and Tom could not see where the armour finished or where Bloodboar began.

My blade will never be able to cut through that, Tom thought desperately. *How will I defeat him?*

"I've an idea," Elenna said urgently, as she watched the Beast lumbering towards them.

"We need to lure Bloodboar – make him charge us. He's tough, but he's not quick. If we can get out of his path in time, he'll tire out eventually."

Tom nodded. "Alright but we stay together as one target, we'll only jump apart at the last moment."

"Agreed," Elenna said, nodding.

They faced the Beast as he charged

towards them – the ground trembling beneath their feet. Tom had to fight the urge to run to meet Bloodboar. He could see the fury in the Beast's eyes as the huge boar thundered ever closer.

"Now!" At the last moment, Tom and Elenna separated and leapt out of the way.

As Tom tumbled across the ground, he saw a glimpse of Bloodboar's hairy hide charging past. It was covered with filth and mud but, most importantly, Tom could see that the armour did not grow from the Beast's skin – it sat on top, like a casing. *If I can get close enough I might be able to prise the armour off*, Tom thought excitedly. *Then Bloodboar will be vulnerable.*

Tom scrambled to his feet. Elenna

joined him. Bloodboar stopped and in a slow circle stomped round to face them. But this time he did not charge. He stalked forwards, his yellow, glowing eyes focused on Tom.

"I think he's worked out our plan," Tom said, taking a step back. "This Beast is too clever to go charging about until he's exhausted." He felt a surge of anxiety as he took another step back and found himself against one of the palace walls. "You have to go, Elenna. This Beast only wants to fight me. If I face him, I might be able to defeat him. Go and help tackle the pirates!"

Elenna shook her head stubbornly. "I'm not leaving you," she said.

"Listen to him," Taladon called from the battlements of the city. "Tom should fight Bloodboar alone."

Elenna nodded. "Alright Tom, good

luck. I know you can do this."

His friend edged away. She watched Bloodboar in case he decided to attack her. But the Beast's gaze never left Tom's.

"Come on then," Tom cried. "What are you waiting for?"

With a snort, Bloodboar lowered his tusks and charged.

Tom raised his sword and ran out to meet him. With a cry, he leapt up onto one of the Beast's tusks and then ran up his face, using ridges in the bone armour's faceplate for his feet to get a grip. Once balanced on Bloodboar's head he somersaulted onto the Beast's back, being careful to place his feet between the spikes that stuck out from the Beast's body.

Bending his knees to keep steady, Tom shoved the point of his sword beneath Bloodboar's armour and tried to prise it up. If he could make the armour fall away, this would finally be a fair fight.

Bloodboar reared up onto his hind legs and spun round trying to dislodge Tom from his back. Gritting his teeth Tom held onto one of the Beast's spikes and continued to try and wedge his sword beneath the armour. With an angry bellow, Bloodboar charged forward and slammed his body into a wall, sending Tom leaping up into the air.

Tom's sword slipped from where it was lodged in Bloodboar's armour and he felt his body spinning through the air. He hit the ground with a painful thud and everything went black.

CHAPTER FOUR

ELENNA'S PLAN

"Tom!" Elenna's scream dragged him from unconsciousness.

He woke to the rasping sound of his own gasps for air. Tom groaned and opened his eyes. His cheek was pressed against cold flagstones, which trembled as something charged towards him.

Bloodboar.

Ignoring the pain in his ribs, Tom stumbled to his feet. To his left he could see his sword and, ducking down, he grabbed it. Standing ready, he thrust his blade forwards as Bloodboar attacked again.

The Beast snorted angrily as Tom jabbed the sword beneath his face armour and almost blinded him.

With a roar, Bloodboar whipped his head from side to side, pulling painfully on Tom's arms, before twisting the blade away from his face and staggering backwards. There was a trickle of blood on the Beast's skin that gave Tom hope. *So I can* make an impact!

Bloodboar's sides heaved and he was slick with sweat beneath the armour. Tom followed his movements carefully as the Beast took another step back. Bloodboar may have been out of breath but he was not done yet.

Tom dared to risk a quick look behind him. Sanpao's ship was gradually moving through the air to cover the courtyard. King Hugo's men were running out of missiles and the rain of arrows had become a trickle.

The Beast snorted again, his yellow eyes combing the courtyard. As he spotted the Tree of Being, he began pawing the ground with one of his sharp hooves and charged forwards.

With a cry, Tom jumped in front of him. He saw Elenna run across the courtyard and snatch two spears from the soldiers who stood nearby.

"What are you doing?" Tom called out, his sword raised ready to battle the Beast.

"You just focus on distracting Bloodboar," Elenna shouted.

Tom nodded and swung his sword down as the Beast tried to ram into him.

Bloodboar gave a scream of agony; Tom's sword had sliced off the tip of one of his mighty tusks. The Beast recoiled and reared up, his sharp hooves kicking out as he tried to stomp down on Tom.

Ducking out of the way of Bloodboar's muscular legs, Tom jumped back. Enraged, the Beast stalked after him. *If Bloodboar's focussed on me, at least it means the Tree of Being is safe*, he thought.

He heard a fierce clash of swords and turned to see King Hugo's men push forward as one unit, meeting the pirates of Makai, blade to blade, blow for blow. He just hoped they could hold back Sanpao's men for long enough.

"Tom, over here!" Elenna shouted out.

He looked to one side and saw that his friend had connected the two spears with a long length of rope. Tom frowned. He still couldn't work out what she was planning, but he started to back away in her direction.

Elenna lifted one of the spears, testing the weight in her hand "Get ready to run as fast as you can," she told Tom. "You need to get Bloodboar to chase after you at full speed. It's the only way this plan will work."

Tom nodded, suddenly understanding what Elenna's plan was.

"That shouldn't be too hard," Tom called back. "Bloodboar wants to catch me!"

Tom led Bloodboar away from Elenna and as the Beast bore down on him, he struck his sword against the Beast's faceplate so even the hilt of his weapon trembled.

Sheathing his blade, Tom sprinted away again and Bloodboar let out an enraged bellow, surging after him.

"Now!" Elenna cried and threw the spear towards Tom. He caught it, spun on his heel and ran in the opposite direction to Elenna.

Behind him, Tom could feel Bloodboar's foul breath on his neck. The Beast was gaining on him, the tip of a tusk tearing at his clothes. Gripping the spear tightly, Tom lowered his head and pumped his legs even harder, finding a reserve of speed he didn't know he had.

Twang! The rope pulled taut. Tom stopped and crouched low. Across the courtyard, he could see Elenna doing the same thing. Between them they had created a tripwire.

Bloodboar's thundering steps made the ground shudder and Tom stared at the charging Beast. His yellow eyes

widened and he let out a snort of
terror as he spotted the rope. He tried
to slow himself by driving his hooves
into the dust but it was too late. The
Beast's momentum carried him
forward and his thick forelegs caught
on the rope.

Tom tensed his muscles and
tightened his hold, as the spear was

almost ripped from his hands. On the other side of the courtyard, he could see that Elenna was clenching her teeth with effort. Her arms trembled, but she managed to hold onto her spear.

With an angry snarl, the Beast slammed into the ground with a bone-shaking thud. Bloodboar lay still for a moment, stunned, but then with a loud, creaking sound the Beast tried to raise his head. But he was caught on something and began snorting in panic and rage.

Tom looked closer. The Beast's tusks had stabbed into the stone ground, holding him fast. The Beast kicked his legs, trying to work himself free.

"Elenna, come and look," Tom called.

His friend bounded over, her face

flooding with relief.

"He's trapped," she said. "The plan worked. We've defeated him!"

Several of the soldiers who stood nearby clapped enthusiastically.

Bloodboar snorted in panic, jerking his head from side to side. But he couldn't free his tusks. His movements became more frenzied and with a snap, the bone faceplate was pulled off his head. Without his armour, Bloodboar looked strangely vulnerable, the skin beneath his hair was pale and soft.

Tom drew his sword but Bloodboar was no longer struggling to free himself from the ground. Without his armoured faceplate, Bloodboar seemed to be drained of all power. Tom stared into Bloodboar's eyes and saw something like relief in their

golden depths. His skin dried and
became grey, as if his whole body
was made of ash. There was a gust
of wind and the Beast collapsed into
a heap of dust. The breeze blew
again and gathered up the remains
of the Beast.

Tom and Elenna watched as the wind carried Bloodboar away. They had won the fight.

The only thing that was left behind was a small fragment of bone in the shape of a star. Tom picked it up.

"It must be your next token," Elenna said.

"That was a brave Beast," Tom said, tucking the star into his sash. He struggled to find any happiness in his heart at defeating the sixth Beast of Sanpao. The Pirate King had controlled the Beasts through the stolen branch of the Tree of Life that made the main mast on his pirate ship. He'd never had any natural born power over these animals.

"I hate Sanpao," Tom muttered. "What right does he have to control Beasts like this?"

Elenna placed a hand on his arm. "It's too late for the Beasts. But not for Avantia, and not for Freya."

"You're right." Tom nodded. "And now I have a token, which means more power against Sanpao. Where is he?" He scanned the courtyard. "Where's my enemy?"

CHAPTER FIVE

WHEN PIRATES ATTACK

A deep, full throated laugh rumbled through the air.

"You may have defeated Bloodboar, Tom, but you cannot stop me." Sanpao's cruel voice bellowed through his war-horn. "You and your father will perish on this day. The Pirates of Makai will seize the Tree of Being!"

Tom looked up to see that Sanpao's ship was hovering directly over the city. The archers on the city walls had run out of arrows and could only watch as several boats were heaved overboard and hordes of pirates lowered themselves into the courtyard.

"Find a weapon! Replenish your arrows! FIGHT!" King Hugo cried, urging his men off the battlements. "Avantia will be victorious."

Tom faced the band of pirates with his sword and shield held high.

Elenna stood ready, one of the spears she used to defeat Bloodboar gripped in her hand.

"Surround the tree," Tom shouted to the Avantian soldiers. "We must protect it at all costs."

Tom, Elenna and King Hugo's men backed towards the tree, creating a defensive circle. Taladon stood nearby, handing out swords, spears and maces.

"If Sanpao wants this tree, he'll have to get through us," Elenna growled. The soldiers roared in agreement.

Tom tightened his hold on his sword as he saw the tide of pirates surge towards them. One pirate swirled a pair of whips in the air and grinned as he brought it cracking onto the ground, splitting the courtyard's flagstone. Another held a hammer studded with sharp metal spikes in one hand and a net in the other.

Whilst there's blood in my veins I will not let them take the Tree, Tom vowed.

A soldier with long dark hair held two short swords and swivelled them in her palms before lunging to meet the pirate who leapt at her. "Avantia, Avantia!" she whooped as she disarmed the pirate and sent him running for his life.

The bandit with the whips came after Tom, his weapon lashing out

with a hiss. Tom raised his sword in
an arc and cut through the thick
leather lash.

"You'll pay for that, boy," the pirate
growled and with a flick of his wrist
sent his other whip lashing out
towards Tom's sword hand.

Tom cried out as the leather cut
his hand and he dropped his sword.

A flare of anger replaced the pain and Tom swiftly grabbed the end of the whip and pulled on it with all his might. The pirate staggered forward and as he tried to regain his balance, Tom leaped towards him. He swiftly weaved in and out around the pirate, tying him up with the whip. With a push from Tom, the man fell to the ground like an oak tree cut at its base.

As the pirate lay wriggling in the dirt, trying to break his bonds, Tom grabbed his sword. The bandit's eyes widened in fear.

"Don't worry. I won't finish you while you lay helpless," Tom said. He turned his back on the pirate and entered into the battle once more. He could see Elenna fighting a man with a long, curved cutlass. His friend never took her eyes from the blade in her opponent's hand and lunged and then blocked with her spear until she knocked the weapon from the pirate's grasp.

Elenna grinned as the pirate turned tail and ran. Tom and his friend stood shoulder to shoulder as two more pirates came at them.

The pirate with the net and spiked hammer was suddenly upon Tom, his eyes blazing with bloodlust. He swung his spiked hammer and Tom ducked, one of the spikes grazing the top of his head.

As Tom got ready to stand once again, he felt a whoosh of air and then something heavy and knotted landed on him and immediately pulled tight.

The net, Tom thought.

"Oh, what's this?" the pirate

mocked. "I've caught myself a little fishy. I'd better put it out of its misery."

Tom struggled inside the net. He could hear the pirate's approaching footsteps, then his feet were suddenly in view. He tried to use his sword to cut through the net's thick strands, but it was covered in some kind of tar, and his blade kept slipping off.

The pirate loomed over him and with a cry brought down his spiked hammer. With a jerk, Tom managed to roll out of the way.

He tried to untangle himself. Frustration made his hands sweat and his heart pound.

"You're not going get away, little fishy," the pirate crowed. "Do us all a favour and keep still, so I can

pound your head in good and proper."

Out of the corner of his eye, Tom saw a glint of the metal hammer head and he swiftly rolled in the other direction as the pirate's weapon came smashing down.

"Hey you!" Elenna yelled at the hammer wielding pirate. Tom glanced over and saw that the other pirate she'd been battling had been swiftly relieved of his weapon.

"Why don't you fight someone who isn't tied up?" Elenna said "Or are you too much of a coward?"

With a roar of anger, the pirate turned from Tom and charged towards Elenna. She met him bravely but as she used her spear to deflect the blows from the pirate's hammer, Tom saw a wiry pirate lowering himself from one of Sanpao's lifeboats, just above Elenna's head.

"Elenna, watch out!" he cried, still struggling to get out of the net. But it was too late. The pirate dropped onto Elenna's shoulders and wrapped his legs around her throat.

With a choked gasp, she dropped to her knees. with her hands clawing at the pirate's legs. Her face was turning red; she couldn't breathe.

Elenna was being strangled to death!

CHAPTER SIX

THE TIDE OF BATTLE

Tom continued to struggle in the net, tearing at the ropes that imprisoned him. The pirate with the hammer smiled up at his friend who was choking Elenna.

"That's right, squeeze the breath right out of her," he growled.

Terror cut through Tom's frustration and cleared his mind. *I know what I've got to do.*

He needed to get past the tar on the net. He stopped fighting against his bonds and manoeuvred his shield round, using the edge to scrape away the tar. A patch of unprotected rope appeared and he slashed with his sword. Yes! It cut straight through the hessian.

Untangling himself and springing to his feet, he hurled his shield at the pirate who was choking Elenna. The shield flew through the air in a tight arc and hit the man on his temple before swooping round to return to Tom. The pirate looked dazed, released his grip on Elenna's neck and toppled backwards. He lay unconscious on the flagstone floor.

The pirate with the spiked hammer whirled round. "It looks like my little fishy has escaped." He stalked towards Tom.

Tom scooped the tar from the edge of the shield and flicked the gunky mess into the pirate's face.

"Aaahhh! My eyes!" the pirate bellowed. "You rotten dog, you've blinded me." He dropped his hammer and fell to his knees trying to wipe the tar from his face.

Tom ran over to Elenna who was rubbing her neck. "Are you alright?" he asked.

"I think so," Elenna voice was hoarse and her face was red. She bent down to pick up her spear and quickly looked around. "Listen, stop worrying about me. We've got to protect the Tree."

Tom and Elenna fell back into the circle that surrounded the Tree of Being. The soldier with the long dark hair smiled grimly at them.

"It's getting harder and harder to hold these pirates back," she told them, shaking her head bitterly. "My swords are nearly completely blunt from all the fighting."

Elenna held out her spear. "Take this."

"What about you?" the soldier asked.

Elenna brought her bow and arrow round her body. "I was saving my arrows, but I think the time has come to use them."

The pirates were now a flood, pushing all together. As one pirate was defeated, another immediately took his place. Sanpao remained on the floating ship but with his war-horn began to chant.

"Parry, duck, thrust and slice,
Hack them down, don't think twice."

Pirates joined in with the chanting
and continued to try and break
through the circle that protected
the Tree.

Tom slashed out with his sword,
being careful to protect his body with
his shield. He could see Elenna
darting here and there, releasing
arrows from her bow. King Hugo

and the injured Taladon were fighting as well. Tom had never seen the king fight before, and was impressed with his speed and skill. The king kept his elbows bent, and close to his body, which meant he could thrust and parry much more quickly than his opponents. He felled pirate after pirate, never tiring. Tom felt even more pride for his father. Despite his injuries, he was twice the swordsman of any of Sanpao's men. But King Hugo's men were still outnumbered by the ruthless pirates.

What are we going to do? Tom thought.

There had to be a way to turn the tide of battle. For a moment he wished he could be on Storm's back, riding through the pirates, pushing them back.

Yes, that was it! Putting his fingers

to his mouth, he whistled loudly.

There was a clatter of hooves and a furious whinny. It was Storm and Blizzard!

The two horses galloped into the mass of bodies. They were without saddles and must have come straight from the palace stables. The horses swept their heads from side to side, bucking and kicking their legs, scattering the pirates everywhere.

"Follow me," Tom called out to the others. "I have a plan." He ran forwards eagerly, and leapt onto his stallion's back. Taladon climbed up behind him. Elenna and King Hugo scrambled onto Blizzard, and together, all four of them cut deep paths into the pirate swarm.

Elenna released more arrows while Tom, Taladon and King Hugo swung

their swords down at the pirates,
their blades meeting daggers and
cutlasses in showers of sparks.

Sanpao's men snarled in fury, their
sweaty, red faces twisted with rage as
they tried to fight back – but now
they were the ones at a disadvantage.

The Avantian soldiers didn't waste
a moment. The soldier with Elenna's

spear swung it at the retreating pirates, tripping them up and making them fall to the ground. Other soldiers charged with their weapons, driving the pirates further away.

As the tide of battle turned in the favour of King Hugo's men, Sanpao's voice sounded on the air again.

"Tom, you may be winning this time, but there will always be other fights." Sanpao twirled his weapon above his head, his muscles flexing under oiled, tattooed skin. His scarred face split in a wicked smile. "You have not seen the last of the Pirate King!"

"No," Tom cried as he saw the pirate ship turn around and heave through the air.

Sanpao, the most evil man to ever visit Avantia, was escaping.

CHAPTER SEVEN

ON THE EDGE

Tom heard a cry. Looking down from Storm's back, he saw a pirate staring up at the sky.

"King Sanpao," the pirate wailed. "Please don't leave us."

His plea was echoed by several other pirates as they dropped their weapons and held up their hands in surrender.

Tom felt just as desperate as the pirates. *If only there was a way to stop him*, Tom thought. *If only…*

Whoosh!

A bolt of brilliant turquoise light shot across the sky. The light surrounded the ship, holding it in place.

Tom followed the blue beam to its source and felt a smile spread across his face as he saw Aduro standing in the middle of the courtyard. The wizard looked stronger than before, and he wore a brand new turquoise robe that crackled with magic.

Tom's breath came out as a gasp. "What has happened to Aduro?" he asked, turning in the saddle to look at his father.

"Aduro used up almost all of his magic to fight off the spell that

Sanpao put on him," Taladon explained. "It almost killed him – but, instead of dying he has been reborn as an even stronger wizard. I've heard legends where this has happened, but never seen it. Aduro is more powerful than ever before!"

Tom whipped back round to face Aduro.

"Your reign of terror is at an end, Sanpao," the Good Wizard called. He turned his hands over and over, reeling in the Pirate King's ship on an invisible beam of magic.

Sanpao no longer had control of his ship. His snarls of fury could be heard all round the courtyard as he leaned over the side and sent furious curses down to the wizard.

As the ship continued to be lowered, Sanpao tried to scramble up

one of the mast poles. Tom laughed.
"What good will that do?" he called
out. "Where do you think you're
going to go?"

With a flick of his hand, Aduro
forced the ship to land on the

battlements of the city. The pirates in the courtyard gasped and cowered as the ship skidded along the ramparts, crashing into a wing of the palace. It teetered dangerously on the edge. Sanpao climbed down from the mast but he had nowhere left to run.

"Finish your Beast Quest, Tom," Taladon murmured in his ear.

Tom jumped off Storm and ran across the courtyard. Many of the pirates had now surrendered and King Hugo's men had gathered them into groups. Both soldiers and pirates watched as Tom raced over to the battlements.

He ran up the stairs two at time. Up on the city walls, the wind whipped at his hair and howled all around him. Ahead, he could see the Pirate King's ship see-sawing in the strong breeze as it balanced on the city's walls.

Tom climbed onto the ship and aimed the point of his sword at Sanpao. "We have unfinished business," he yelled. "Come here and fight me."

Sanpao's face twisted into a mask of rage. Drawing his cutlass, he traced the blade with his finger, grinning wolfishly. "This blade is sharp enough to cut you in two, boy, and that's exactly what I'm going to do."

Sanpao lunged, but Tom was ready for him and swung his sword, meeting the Pirate King's heavier weapon with a deafening clang. Tom twisted his wrist and with a nimble movement flicked Sanpao's cutlass out of his hand. The Pirate King's weapon spun across the deck and onto the plank that jutted from the far side of the ship. Sanpao scurried after it, with Tom right behind him.

As Tom stepped onto the plank, he felt the wood flex beneath him. His stomach rolled, as he peered over the edge. The length of wood extended far off the side of the battlements, and hung over empty space. It was a long way down...

Swallowing hard, Tom tried to keep his balance. Sanpao now had his sword. With an ugly sneer he strode forward, his weight making the plank quiver. The ship tilted even more dangerously.

"Sanpao, just surrender. It's not safe on this plank," Tom said urgently.

"Never," Sanpao snarled. With a cry he ran towards Tom and lifted his cutlass to strike, but Tom swiftly

parried the attack, pushing the
pirate away.

The Pirate King took one step back,
and then another, and another, as he
attempted to steady himself.

"Watch out," Tom called. But the
Pirate King was right on the edge of
the plank, his arms flailing as he tried
to keep his balance.

Tom lunged forward to help the
pirate. He may have wanted to defeat
Sanpao but he didn't want to kill
him. Tom grabbed onto the jewelled
belt around Sanpao's waist. He'd
been without his belt ever since
Sanpao had stolen it at the beginning
of this Quest.

For a moment, Sanpao regained his
balance but then the belt ripped itself
free and Sanpao toppled backwards,
his face rigid with fear.

"Sanpao!" Tom cried as the Pirate King disappeared over the side of the ship.

CHAPTER EIGHT

THE DARK PATH

A rush of guilt rose up inside Tom. There was no way someone could survive a fall from such a height. Tom closed his eyes, trying to block out the vision of Sanpao's terrified face, but a bright blue light pierced his eyelids. He peered out. In front of him Sanpao was floating, encased in an orb of blue light. Then the orb descended, lowering Sanpao into the middle of the courtyard. Aduro stood in front of him.

"You used your magic to save him!" Tom called down. Aduro smiled.

Tom scrambled back onto the deck of the ship. From up high, he saw Sanpao fall to his knees. Taladon and Hugo were the first to surround him, swords drawn. Elenna followed behind, her arrow trained on the leader of the pirates.

"Just finish it, Taladon," Sanpao cried, bending his head and pulling his oiled plait away from his neck. "Kill me."

Taladon shook his head. "No, I will not slay you in cold blood," Tom heard his father say. "Lay your cutlass to one side and change your ways, Sanpao. Anyone can turn from a dark path, if they can find the strength from within."

Sanpao nodded slowly before throwing his cutlass aside.

Taladon sheathed his sword, extended a hand to Sanpao and pulled the Pirate King to his feet. For a moment it almost looked like they were shaking hands.

Shaking hands. Tom suddenly remembered the vision he saw in the

Eye of Kronus – the moving images had showed Sanpao stabbing his father!

Down below, the Pirate King reached into one of his boots.

He pulled out a dagger.

Moving instinctively, Tom took the bone star from his sash and threw it down towards the courtyard. It wheeled through the air before slamming into the pirate's blade hand. Sanpao screamed in pain, dropping the weapon.

The bone star faded away and Tom smiled. Another magic Beast token put to good use!

"Bind him," King Hugo ordered his soldiers. Sanpao was helpless as Taladon drew his sword again and pointed it at him while the soldiers bound his hands with rope. *He had his chance and he wasted it*, Tom thought.

The pirate king was led away. But as he struggled in the grip of soldiers, he craned his head back to send Tom one last evil glance. *This isn't over*, it seemed to say.

Tom looked around. Most of the pirates had been rounded up, but a few others had escaped and raced beyond the city walls, melting away into the kingdom.

Tom sighed. It wouldn't be an easy job to hunt them down and recapture them. He climbed off the ship and dropped back down to the ground using a length of rope.

"Thank you, my son." Taladon said as Tom approached. "You saved my life *and* Avantia. And it's not the first time! You are a true hero."

Tom bowed his head. "I'm just pleased we managed to protect the

Tree of Being." His gaze fell on the mighty tree. It looked even more magnificent, with its sturdy trunk and emerald green leaves. What was once a broken, gnarled tree was now strong and gloriously alive with magic. "This is what the whole Quest has been for," he said. "Protecting it."

But will the tree really bring back Silver, or reunite me with my mother? he thought.

"It's time to find out, don't you think?" Elenna asked, coming to stand by his side.

"How do you always know what I'm thinking?" Tom asked, staring at his friend who looked tired from the battle they'd just endured.

Elenna smiled. "We've been on so many Quests with each other. I should hope that I know what you're thinking by now. Come on. I've missed Silver so much, I don't think I can wait much longer."

As they got closer to the Tree of Being, Tom's step faltered.

Elenna slowed as well and looked up at him questioningly.

"This Tree holds all our hopes," Tom murmured. "We fought so hard to protect it. What if it doesn't work? What if it doesn't bring them back—"

A thrashing sound interrupted him. The tree's branches had begun to wave to and fro in the wind and the trunk made a noisy cracking sound as deep splits appeared in its surface. Sap oozed from the wounds.

"Something is wrong," Elenna cried, her voice cracking. "I think the tree is dying. Silver and Freya will never come home!"

CHAPTER NINE

A TRUE HERO OF AVANTIA

Shards of wood flew in every direction as the trunk of the tree continued to crack and split.

With Elenna at his side, Tom rushed forwards. He half expected to see the tree topple over, but within the heart of the tree's trunk an arch formed, as if an invisible artist had taken a blade to the wood and cut a doorway into it. The tree wasn't dying, it was forming a portal!

Tom felt a sharp pain in his arm. He looked down to see that Elenna was gripping it hard.

"Do you think..?" Elenna's fingers dug even more deeply.

"They're coming, Elenna," Tom said. "Silver and Freya are on their way!"

They waited at the archway, expecting Elenna's wolf and Tom's mother to come through it at any moment. But nothing happened. The archway stood empty, a gaping hole that led into a pure black abyss. Soldiers surrounded them, watching silently.

Tom stood right on the brink of the emptiness, his hands gripping the edges of the archway.

"I don't understand," Elenna said from behind him. "The tree's created a gateway for Silver and Freya to return. Why aren't they here?"

Tom peered into darkness, listening hard. Then he heard it – a faint howling that he would recognise anywhere. His heart began to pound. "I think they're coming," he called. Reaching into the abyss, he felt an icy cold creep up his arm.

And then...he felt it. A hand, strong yet soft in his grip. *Mother!* All the way from the land of Tavania, Freya was reaching out for him!

"Elenna, help me," Tom gasped. "I've got Freya. I need to pull her out."

His friend swiftly reached into the abyss and caught hold of the same arm that Tom held. "I can feel it.

I can feel her arm," she cried.

Together, they pulled Freya into
Avantia. With a gasp, the Mistress
of the Beasts tumbled into the
courtyard. With her free hand,
she held onto Silver's neck, guiding
him through the archway.

Tom stared at his mother as she climbed to her feet. His throat felt tight. Freya opened her arms and Tom hugged his mother tight.

"Hello, Mother," he whispered.

"Hello, my son," she murmured back.

With a joyous howl, Silver jumped into Elenna's arms, bowling her over and eagerly licking her face.

Elenna buried her face in Silver's fur, her cheeks wet with tears.

From nearby, Tom could hear Storm give a snort that was both a mixture of happiness and impatience. He turned to look at his horse.

Silver broke away from Elenna and bounded over to Storm, nuzzling his head against Storm's leg. Storm bowed his head and playfully nipped at Silver. The wolf yelped in return, startling Blizzard who stood nearby. Looking at Blizzard in interest, Silver padded over and gave the other horse the same affectionate greeting that Storm had received. Blizzard didn't seem to mind, even though this was the first time that they had met!

With a grin, Tom turned back to his mother, eager to ask her questions, but Freya was looking across the courtyard at Taladon, her face unreadable.

The Master of the Beasts hesitantly walked over to them.

"Hello, Freya," he said.

"It's been…a long time," Tom's mother replied. Freya smiled but Tom could see that her eyes were sad and full of regrets.

Freya shared an awkward hug with Taladon.

"Tom, be careful!" Elenna cried.

But it was too late, a bundle of silver fur barrelled into Tom's chest and he found himself on the floor with a wolf licking his face.

"Hello, boy," Tom said ruffling Silver's fur. "Welcome home."

"Welcome home, indeed," King Hugo said as he joined the group. Aduro stood at his side, his cloak swirling all about him, the fabric sparking with magic.

The king turned to the Mistress of the Beasts. "It has been many years since I saw you last, Freya."

"Indeed." she replied. "A lot has happened, both here and in Tavania."

King Hugo nodded. "That's true. Avantia has suffered many trials. But we have also been gifted a true hero. Your son, Tom."

Freya looked at Tom, her eyes burning with pride.

Aduro smiled. "But no hero can succeed alone. Elenna has been a true warrior and hero as well."

Elenna's cheeks grew rosy as she blushed with pleasure.

Freya looked Aduro up and down. "My dear friend, you look very well. You appear younger than you did the last time I saw you!"

Aduro laughed. "Sanpao's spell was powerful, but what doesn't kill you makes you stronger. I find my power to be twice as strong now."

"I'm pleased," Freya said. "Avantia is lucky to be protected by such a powerful wizard and such brave heroes."

"But what of Tavania?" Tom asked. "Who protects that kingdom? Is it safe?"

Freya smiled proudly. "My son, the kingdom you and Elenna helped to save on your last Quest is now thriving. However, I mus—"

A rumbling sound interrupted her. The Tree of Being was sinking back into the earth. Storm tossed his head nervously as the noise continued to boom round the courtyard. Silver howled in protest.

Tom took a step back from the Tree as the earth trembled beneath his feet. "Aduro, what does this mean?" he shouted over the noise.

"Don't worry," Aduro called back. "The Tree will return when needed." As the Tree's branches sank out of sight and the earth closed up, Tom heard an almighty crash behind him.

He whipped round. Sanpao's pirate ship had slipped off the ramparts and smashed into the building below.

The palace dungeon! Tom realised.

"We must save those prisoners,"
King Hugo called.

"Lift the rubble, soldiers!" Taladon
commanded. "Quickly, before it's too
late."

Immediately, Tom, Elenna, Freya
and Aduro joined the soldiers along
with King Hugo and Taladon, and
dug people out of the rubble.

They lifted the heavy stone bricks
in silence. Silver yelped and pawed
at a piece of rubble.

Gritting his teeth, Tom moved the
rock out of the way. A hand reached
up to him and Tom pulled on it,
freeing the prisoner.

Tom felt himself being pushed
backwards as the prisoner made
a break for it. Who would be so

ungrateful? He only caught a flash of the face before the figure was out of reach.

Malvel.

Tom leapt to his feet and dashed after him.

"Tom, stop," Aduro said. "There are still many people trapped. Malvel and others may have escaped, but there

are still people to save."

"But what if he tries to seize power again?" Tom asked.

Aduro smiled grimly. "There were times when I didn't think I'd be able to recover from Sanpao's spell, but as I fought for life I realised something: there is always a new evil to defeat. There will always be enemies."

Tom felt Aduro's hand on his shoulder as he stared into the distance. He could no longer make out Malvel's figure. If the Evil Wizard ever tried to take over Avantia again, Tom knew he would be there to challenge him.

Tom had managed to defeat six of Sanpao's evil Beasts. He'd never turn away from danger – especially now that his mother had returned.
He wanted to make her proud.

Freya, Taladon and Aduro drew
near, while Elenna came to stand
at Tom's side.

"Whatever new adventures await us," Tom vowed. "Together we will be ready."

Don't miss Tom's next
Beast Quest
adventure!

Win an exclusive
Beast Quest T-shirt and goody bag!

In every Beast Quest book the Beast Quest logo is hidden in
one of the pictures. Find the logos in books 43 to 48
and make a note of which pages they appear on. Write the
six page numbers on a postcard and send it in to us.
Each month we will draw one winner to receive
a Beast Quest T-shirt and goody bag.

THE BEAST QUEST COMPETITION:
THE PIRATE KING
Orchard Books
338 Euston Road, London NW1 3BH
Australian readers should email:
childrens.books@hachette.com.au

New Zealand readers should write to:
Beast Quest Competition
4 Whetu Place, Mairangi Bay, Auckland, NZ
or email: childrensbooks@hachette.co.nz

Only one entry per child.
Final draw: 4 March 2012

You can also enter this competition
via the Beast Quest website: www.beastquest.co.uk

Join the Quest,
Join the Tribe

www.beastquest.co.uk

Have you checked out the Beast Quest website? It's the place to go for games, downloads, activities, sneak previews and lots of fun!

You can read all about your favourite beasts, download free screensavers and desktop wallpapers for your computer, and even challenge your friends to a Beast Tournament.

Sign up to the newsletter at www.beastquest.co.uk to receive exclusive extra content and the opportunity to enter special members-only competitions. We'll send you up-to-date info on all the Beast Quest books, including the next exciting series which features six brand-new Beasts!

All books priced at £4.99,
special bumper editions
priced at £5.99.

Orchard Books are available from all good bookshops, or can
be ordered from our website: www.orchardbooks.co.uk,
or telephone 01235 827702, or fax 01235 8227703.

Series 8: THE PIRATE KING
COLLECT THEM ALL!

Sanpao the Pirate King wants to steal the sacred Tree of Being. Can Tom scupper his plans?

978 1 40831 310 7

978 1 40831 311 4

978 1 40831 312 1

978 1 40831 313 8

978 1 40831 314 5

978 1 40831 315 2

Series 9: The Warlock's Staff
Out September 2011

Meet six terrifying new Beasts!

Ursus the Clawed Roar
Minos the Demon Bull
Koraka the Winged Assassin
Silver the Wild Terror
Spikefin the Water King
Torpix the Twisting Serpent

Watch out for the next Special Bumper Edition

OUT OCT 2011!

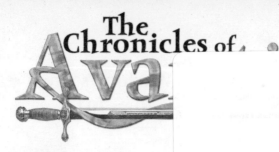

The Chronicles of Avantia

FROM TH
A HERO

Dare to enter the kingdom of Avantia.

A new evil arises in Avantia. Lord Derthsin has ordered his armies into the four corners of Avantia. If the four Beasts of Avantia can find their Chosen Riders they might have the strength to challenge Derthsin. But if they fail, the land of Avantia will be lost forever…

FIRST HERO, CHASING EVIL AND CALL TO WAR, OUT NOW!
Fire and Fury out July 2011